A Gift For:

Allyson

From:

~~I have no ida~~

mom

Published by Hallmark Gift Books,
a division of Hallmark Cards, Inc.,
Kansas City, MO 64141
Visit us on the Web at www.Hallmark.com.

Editor: Megan Langford
Art Director: Kevin Swanson
Designer: Scott Swanson
Production Designer: Bryan Ring

ISBN: 978-1-59530-468-1
BOK1189

Printed and bound in China
NOV11

My Pet Giraffe

By Linda Staten
Illustrated by Paul Nicholls

Hallmark

GIFT BOOKS

This is my pet giraffe. His name is Goldie. Goldie is my very best friend. He's my tallest friend, too!

Goldie lives in our backyard. Mom says I can't have a giraffe in my room. But I don't mind.

With Goldie, every day is an adventure.

No matter what, there's always something to do.

We play lots of games together. Goldie
is really good at hide-and-seek.

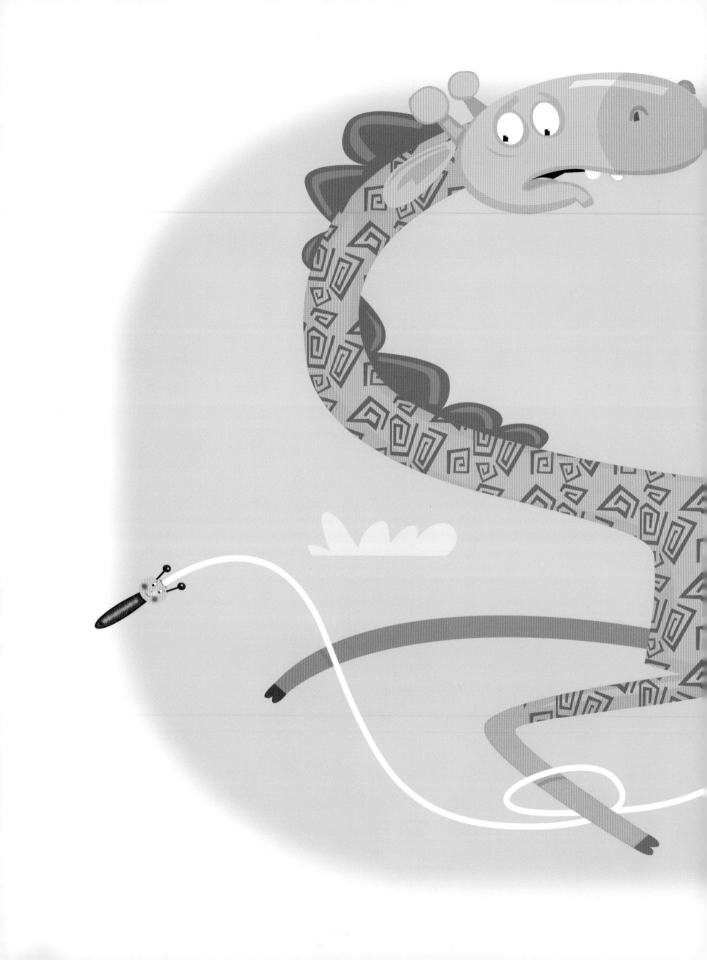

But he's not so good
at jumping rope!

My pet giraffe is smart. He knows lots of tricks, like "sit" . . .

. . . and "lie down."

But I wish I had never taught him how to fetch!

Sometimes I take
Goldie for a walk.

Sometimes he walks me.

And sometimes we have
a party just for us.

Goldie and I make a great team.

I can reach way down low . . .

. . . and Goldie can reach way up high.

Even chores can be fun when
you do them with a friend.

When chores are done, it's bath time.

Goldie loves getting a bath.

Lucky for me, I love getting a shower.

At the end of the day, we like to read together.

Goldie loves funny stories most of all.

If you like to laugh, you should get a giraffe.

I love my pet giraffe. And I just know Goldie and I are going to be friends forever and ever and ever.

Did you like this book?
We would love to hear from you!

Please send your comments to:
Hallmark Book Feedback
P.O. Box 419034
Mail Drop 215
Kansas City, MO 64141

Or e-mail us at:
booknotes@hallmark.com